FUNNY BUNNIES
UP and DOWN

DAVID MELLING

Hodder
Children's
Books

Funny bunny UP,

funny bunny DOWN.

funny bunny FUNNY,

funny bunny FROWN.

Funny bunny MESSY,

Funny bunny CLEAN,

often NICE,

but sometimes MEAN.

Funny bunny
PUSH,

funny bunny PULL,

funny bunny
EMPTY,

funny bunny FULL.

Funny bunny FAST,

funny bunny SLOW,

funny bunny YES,

funny bunny NO.

Funny bunnies PLAY

and funny bunnies FIGHT,

bounce all
DAY and...

Snore all NIGHT.

HODDER CHILDREN'S BOOKS
First published in Great Britain in 2014 by Hodder Children's Books
This paperback edition published in 2019 by Hodder and Stoughton
in association with Scottish Book Trust

A CIP catalogue record for this book is available from the British Library.

ISBN: 978 1 444 95086 1

1 3 5 7 9 10 8 6 4 2

Printed and bound in China

FSC
www.fsc.org
MIX
Paper from
responsible sources
FSC® C104740

Hodder Children's Books
An imprint of Hachette Children's Group
Part of Hodder and Stoughton
Carmelite House
50 Victoria Embankment
London EC4Y 0DZ

An Hachette UK Company
www.hachette.co.uk

www.hachettechildrens.co.uk

www.davidmelling.co.uk